When Charlie McButton Lost Power

SUZANNE COLLINS

Illustrated by MIKE LESTER

PUFFIN BOOKS

PUFFIN BOOKS
Published by the Penguin Group
Penguin Young Readers Group. 345 Hudson Street. New York. New York 10014. U.S.A.
Penguin Group (Canada). 90 Eglinton Avenue East. Suite 700.
Toronto. Ontario. Canada M4P 2Y3 (a division of Pearson Penguin Canada Inc.)
Penguin Books Ltd. 80 Strand. London WC2R 0RL. England
Penguin Ireland. 25 St Stephen's Green. Dublin 2. Ireland (a division of Penguin Books Ltd)
Penguin Group (Australia). 250 Camberwell Road. Camberwell. Victoria 3124. Australia
(a division of Pearson Australia Group Pty Ltd)
Penguin Books India Pvt Ltd. 11 Community Centre.
Panchsheel Park. New Delhi · 110017. India
Penguin Group (NZ). 67 Apollo Drive. Rosedale. North Shore 0745. Auckland. New Zealand
(a division of Pearson New Zealand Ltd)
Penguin Books (South Africa) (Pty) Ltd. 24 Sturdee Avenue. Rosebank.
Johannesburg 2196. South Africa

Registered Offices: Penguin Books Ltd. 80 Strand. London WC2R 0RL. England

First published in the United States of America by G. P. Putnam Sons'. a division of Penguin
Young Readers Group. 2005
Published by Puffin Books. a division of Penguin Young Readers Group. 2007

10 9 8 7 6

THE LIBRARY OF CONGRESS HAS CATALOGED THE G. P. PUTNAM SONS' EDITION AS FOLLOWS:
Collins. Suzanne. When Charlie McButton lost power / Suzanne Collins: illustrated by Mike
Lester. p. cm. Summary: A boy who likes nothing but playing computer games is in trouble when
the power goes out and his little sister has all of the batteries in the house.
[1. Electricity—Fiction. 2. Brothers and sisters—Fiction. 3. Computer games—Fiction.
4. Stories in rhyme.] I. Lester. Mike. ill. II. Title. PZ8.3.C6843 Wh 2005
[E]—dc21 2003001284 ISBN 0-399-24000-4 (hc)

Puffin Books ISBN 978-0-14-240857-5
Design by Gunta Alexander.
Text set in Adriatic.
The art was done with a No. 2 pencil. watercolor. and a Mac.
Manufactured in China

For Charlie and Isabel—S. C.

For Regan—M. L.

Charlie McButton had likes and like-nots.
The things that he liked involved handsets and bots,
Computerized games where he battled bad creatures.
The things he liked-not didn't have blow up features.

Then one day a thunderstorm blew into town
And brought his tech empire tumbling down.
A lightning bolt struck an electrical tower,
And Charlie McButton?

His whole world lost power.

He looked left, he looked right, and his heart filled with dread.
The TV, the lights and his clock were all dead.

He jumped to his feet, his lungs gasping for air.
The room spun around and he clung to his chair.

He tried to cry "Help!" but just managed a squeak.
The blackout had blacked out his power to speak.
Thank goodness his mother had ears like a bat.
She came to his room and she gave him a pat.

HELP!

"Oh, Charlie," she said, picking up on his fears,

"The lights will come back when the bad weather clears.

You'll have to find something without plugs to play.

Read a book!

Clean your room!

Sing a song!

Model clay!"

Could *anything* be any duller than clay?

Soggy gray clay on a soggy gray day?

He hated the way clay got under his nails

And how he could only make snowmen and snails.

He dove for a gadget he'd outgrown last spring.

It was handheld, outdated, not much of a thing.

But he clutched the old toy like a lifeline that day.

See, it ran on one battery. The size? Triple-A.

He flicked the On/Off switch to On double quick,
But no happy humming sound followed the click.
He unlatched a hatch and his blood turned to ice.
"The battery is gone from my backup device!"

World records were set in the ten-meter dash
As away down the hallway he flew like a flash,
Seeking one battery, just one triple-A
That would rescue one boy from a gray day of clay.

But just when his search nearly drove him insane,
He ran past the bedroom of Isabel Jane.
His three-year-old sister was happily walking
A doll back and forth, and the doll—

it was talking!

Now, dolls didn't talk on their own as a rule.
They needed a power source, some kind of fuel.
In less than a second he'd made his decision.
Call it bad judgment, a real lack of vision.

Somehow his head didn't warn of his folly,
And Charlie McButton . . .

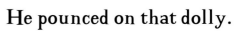

He pounced on that dolly.

He plucked out his prize through the baby doll's dress,
And Isabel Jane made a sound of distress.

It was just a short walk to the foot of the stair
Where resided the McButton time-out time chair.

To add to the fun of his term in the seat,
Isabel Jane came to play at his feet.
And Isabel Jane, the Battery Queen,
Had more triple-A's than he'd ever seen.

They powered her puppies, they powered her clocks,
They powered her talkative alphabet blocks.

Assaulted by nonstop mechanical chatter,
Charlie McButton got madder and madder.

He snapped at his sis from his time-out time zone,
"How come you can't ever
just
leave
me
alone!"

Her eyes filled with tears and she gave them a rub.
She went to the bathroom and hid in the tub.

Then Charlie McButton felt totally rotten
And couldn't help thinking some things he'd forgotten.

Mainly he thought that, for sisters that toddle,
Isabel Jane was a pretty good model.
She clearly adored him. She didn't have fleas.
At dinner she'd secretly eat up his peas.

And sometimes—although he'd most hotly deny it—
He liked to just sit there beside her in quiet.
Wrapped up in a blanket, watching TV,
Her head on his shoulder, her foot on his knee.

He sat and he thought and he stared at the rain.
When his time-out was done, he found Isabel Jane.

From the edge of the tub she gave him a peek,
So he said, "Hey, are we playing hide-and-go-seek?"

She was happy at once and ran into the hall,
As she loved playing hide-and-go-seek most of all.
They took turns being "It" and counting to ten.
They hid in the plants and the guinea pig pen.

And when he found Isabel Jane in her quilt,

They decided a big blanket fort should be built.

Then the gloom made him think about dragons and spells . . .

So Charlie became the great wizard McSmells.

And Isabel Jane, who desired a role,
Magically changed to his faithful old troll.

Between tracking down dragons and brewing up lizards
And handling the day-to-day business of wizards,
Like forging his faithful old troll a new sword,
Charlie McButton forgot to be bored.

At supper they ate under real candlelight.
The daytime had melted right into the night.
And after they'd all been asleep for an hour . . .

The world came alive with a big surge of power.

Oh, it's finally back, Charlie thought with a grin.

Tomorrow I'll wake up and I can plug in!

But another thought hit him he couldn't explain:

I might *also* find dragons with Isabel Jane.